A NOTE TO PARENTS

Reading Aloud with Your Child

Research shows that reading books aloud is the single most valuable support parents can provide in helping children learn to read.

- Be a ham! The more enthusiasm you display, the more your child will enjoy the book.
- Run your finger underneath the words as you read to signal that the print carries the story.
- Leave time for examining the illustrations more closely; encourage your child to find things in the pictures.
- Invite your youngster to join in whenever there's a repeated phrase in the text.
- Link up events in the book with similar events in your child's life.
- If your child asks a question, stop and answer it. The book can be a means to learning more about your child's thoughts.

Listening to Your Child Read Aloud

The support of your attention and praise is absolutely crucial to your child's continuing efforts to learn to read.

- If your child is learning to read and asks for a word, give it immediately so that the meaning of the story is not interrupted. DO NOT ask your child to sound out the word.
- On the other hand, if your child initiates the act of sounding out, don't intervene.
- If your child is reading along and makes what is called a miscue, listen for the sense of the miscue. If the word "road" is substituted for the word "street," for instance, no meaning is lost. Don't stop the reading for a correction.
- If the miscue makes no sense (for example, "horse" for "house"), ask your child to reread the sentence because you're not sure you understand what's just been read.
- Above all else, enjoy your child's growing command of print and make sure you give lots of praise. *You are your child's first teacher—and the most important one. Praise from you is critical for further risk-taking and learning.*

—Priscilla Lynch
Ph.D., New York University
Educational Consultant

To all the children, visible and invisible,
I've met on my travels
—E.L.

For Trinka H. Noble
and all the mysteries of life
— D.B.

Text copyright © 1994 by Elizabeth Levy.
Illustrations copyright © 1994 by Denise Brunkus.
All rights reserved. Published by Scholastic Inc.
HELLO READER! and CARTWHEEL BOOKS
are registered trademarks of Scholastic Inc.

Library of Congress Cataloging-in-Publication Data

Levy, Elizabeth.
   The schoolyard mystery / by Elizabeth Levy : illustrated by Denise Brunkus.
      p.   cm. — (Hello reader! Level 4)
   At head of title: Invisible Inc.
   Summary: Chip, an invisible boy, and his friends solve the mystery of who took the school ball from the playground.
   ISBN 0-590-47483-9
   [1.   Schools — Fiction.   2.   Mystery and detective stories.]
I. Brunkus, Denise, ill.   II. Title.   III. Title: Invisible Inc.--The schoolyard mystery.   IV. Series.
PZ7.L5827Se   1994
[E] —dc20

24 23 22 21 20 19

94-1498
CIP
AC
0 1 2/0

Printed in the U.S.A.   24

First Scholastic printing, September 1994

The Schoolyard Mystery

by Elizabeth Levy

Illustrated by
Denise Brunkus

Hello Reader! — Level 4

SCHOLASTIC INC. Cartwheel ·B·O·O·K·S·®

New York   Toronto   London   Auckland   Sydney

CHAPTER ONE

Tears in the Classroom

Chip Stone walked into his classroom. Bandages covered his face and hands. He looked as if he had been in a giant fire. The whole class gasped, even Keith Broder. Keith was almost never nice to anybody.

Justin's mouth dropped open. Chip was his best friend. He had heard about Chip's accident. Chip looked awful! Chip sat down next to Justin.

Justin scribbled a note that he passed to Chip.

Hey, man, good to have you back!

Chip turned his face to Justin. Justin looked through the bandages but couldn't see Chip's eyes.

He thought he saw a little tear in one corner.

Justin rubbed a tear from his own eye. He sniffled. This pile of bandages was his best friend. Justin would do whatever he could to help Chip get better.

Chip took a pen in his bandaged hand. He could barely hold it. Chip slowly formed each letter. He passed a note to Justin.

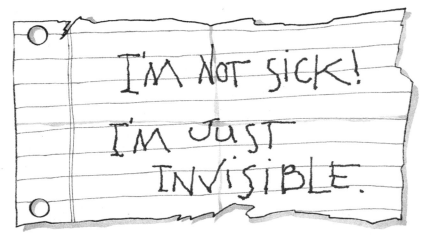

Justin read the note. He wondered if the problem was in Chip's head. Even if it was, he would still stick by his friend.

No matter what.

During recess, the teacher, Mr. Gonshak, brought out a giant rubber ball. It had all the continents and seas on it. It was almost as tall as Mr. Gonshak, and he was six feet.

"The PTO bought this new ball just for the second grade," said Mr. Gonshak. "Isn't it fun? Be careful that Latin America doesn't roll right over you."

The kids shrieked as the ball rolled toward them like a giant bulldozer. Mr. Gonshak went to the swings to talk to Ms. Gerber, the kindergarten teacher.

Keith grabbed the ball and tried
to lift it over his head. It was so big
that he staggered backward and fell.

The ball bounced off his head.
Charlene rolled it away from him.

Keith gave her a dirty look.
Charlene then bounced the ball
toward Justin. It bounced off him. It
was much lighter than it looked.

Justin kicked the ball back to the middle of the group. Chip was standing a little outside of the circle. Justin felt bad. Chip was so heavily bandaged he couldn't play.

Justin walked over to Chip to try

to cheer him up. "Mr. Gonshak is asking Ms. Gerber for a date," Justin said to Chip. Chip giggled through his bandages. He knew all about the times that Justin heard secrets the teachers told each other. Justin couldn't hear well in one ear. His teachers spoke into a special microphone that broadcast straight into a tiny radio Justin wore around his neck. But Mr. Gonshak often forgot to turn the microphone off. Justin heard all kinds of things that he wasn't supposed to. Also, people sometimes forgot that he could read lips.

Then suddenly, Chip walked away like a mummy in his bandages. Justin decided Chip might be lonely.

Justin followed him. Chip turned
a corner by the swings. Then Justin
saw Chip's clothes and a pile of bandages lying on the ground. Had Chip
gone nuts and torn his bandages
off?

"Chip! Chip!" shouted Justin.

Justin felt something clamp over
his mouth but nothing was there!

Justin tried to scream.

"It's me! Chip!" a voice said into Justin's good ear. Justin took a deep breath. The clamp over his mouth felt like a hand. It smelled like Chip. It was warm and human feeling. But Justin couldn't see it!

"Promise not to scream," said the voice.

Justin nodded. Justin felt fingers slowly leaving his mouth. He twirled around to face Chip. But there *was* no Chip! There was just air.

Justin waved his arms in the air. He put his finger out and hit something soft.

"You poked my belly," said Chip.

"Chip?" asked Justin, his voice shaking.

"It's me," said Chip. "In the flesh."

"What flesh?" Justin asked. "I can't see you."

"I know," said Chip. His voice sounded sad. "You can't read my lips. I don't have any lips, but you can hear me, right? I'm talking right into your good ear, okay?"

"I can hear you fine. But what happened to you? Why can't I see you? You can tell me. I'm your friend." Justin reached out to put his arm around Chip's shoulder, but all he got was air. "How did it happen?"

"You know how my mom and dad love to explore caves," said Chip. "We were walking through a cave, and it was dark and a little wet. My foot slipped on some water, and I fell into a pool. I felt cold and wet when I got out, but otherwise I felt fine. It was too dark to see anything in the cave. Then when we came out into the light, Mom was yelling, 'I can hear you, but I can't see you.' She was wailing. I was scared stiff."

"You mean, you didn't break any bones?" said Justin.

"Not a scratch."

Justin stared into the space next to him, trying to figure out where Chip was standing. "This is too weird."

"Weird? *You* think it's weird? Just imagine being *me*. I *feel* fine. But nobody can see me."

"It's easier to see you with the bandages."

"I hate those bandages," said Chip. "The doctor said I should wear them so that kids would treat me normally, but they itch — and nobody treats me normally."

"I'll try," said Justin.

Suddenly, Justin saw something move by the corner of the swings.

"Hey, Justin! Are you reading your own lips? Who are you talking to, dip-lips?" yelled Keith.

Justin rolled his eyes. Keith had such a big mouth, it was easy to read his lips. "Mind your own bees-wax, Keith!" he shouted.

Keith jumped as if he were being

tickled by an invisible hand. He was.

Keith looked at the air next to him. He ran back toward the other kids.

"This could be fun," Chip said just as Mr. Gonshak blew the whistle.

Recess was over. Chip put his bandages back on.

"I'm too old for this," said Justin.

"Old for what?" asked Chip.

"Having an invisible best friend."

CHAPTER TWO
Good Not Evil

"Mom, I'm not wearing the bandages to school," Chip announced when he got home. "It's too hard to talk."

His mother looked worried. "The doctors said that the children in your school may not be ready to accept you as, well . . . different."

"I told Justin what happened to me, and *he* didn't freak," Chip insisted.

The next day Chip put on his clothes and baseball cap — but no bandages.

During show-and-tell, he told the class the truth about what happened.

Charlene raised her hand. "I

think you're very brave," she said.

"Charlene, all I did was trip into a
pool of water in a cave."

"No, I mean to go without your bandages," said Charlene. "To show us who you are."

"He's nothing," said Keith. "He's not even there."

"He is too!" said Justin. "Chip is still the best kid in the class. Three cheers for Chip."

"Hip! Hip! Hooray!" Charlene led the cheering.

The air around Chip's baseball cap turned a slight shade of pink.

"Now that's enough of that," said Mr. Gonshak. "Just because Chip is invisible doesn't mean we may call out in class. Rules are rules."

Then Mr. Gonshak turned toward Mary. "Now, Mary, remember your promise to bring in something for show-and-tell tomorrow."

Mary wouldn't look up. She was very shy. She hardly ever talked in class.

The next day, Mary walked to the front of the room, holding a little cage very tightly. "This is my sala- mander," she whispered. "His name is Doormat because I found him on my doormat."

"Do you want to tell us anything else about him?" asked Mr. Gonshak.

Mary shook her head.

"If you stepped on him, he'd be dead as a doormat," said Keith.

"That's a dormouse, dingbat," said Charlene.

"You mean dead as a doornail," said Justin.

Mary looked horrified. She didn't like the talk about dead salamanders. She held Doormat's cage even tighter.

Mr. Gonshak told her she could take her seat.

Later they were outside in the playground. Mr. Gonshak went to get the ball that looked like the

planet Earth. It was missing.

Mr. Gonshak was very upset. He asked everybody in the class if they had seen it.

"Maybe Chip took it with him to the Bermuda Triangle," said Keith. "Isn't that where everything disappears?"

"Why don't *you* disappear?" yelled Justin.

Mr. Gonshak went to talk to the principal and a group of teachers. "What's he saying?" asked Chip.

"I don't know," said Justin. "He's got the microphone off."

Chip slipped off his jeans and shirt and handed them to Justin. "Here. Hold these. I'll go invisible."

Justin stood there with Chip's clothes in his hands, feeling pretty stupid. He felt even stupider when Charlene came up to him and asked him what he was doing.

A few seconds later, the clothes jumped out of Justin's hands. "Turn around, Charlene! I'm naked," said Chip.

"You're invisible," said Charlene with her hands on her hips.

"Turn around!" hissed Chip. Charlene turned around. Chip quickly slipped his clothes back on.

"The teachers are really mad that the ball is gone. It cost a lot of money. And Ms. Gerber said yes to a date with Mr. Gonshak," said Chip. "Also, Mrs. Gumbel, our old first-grade teacher, is pregnant."

"Chip Stone, you've been eavesdropping!" exclaimed Charlene. "That's terrible. Did the teachers say anything about me?"

"Yeah, they said you're a P-E-T."

"The teacher's pet? Me?" Charlene preened.

"No, Pest Even to Teachers," said Chip.

Charlene pouted.

"He was just kidding," said
Justin. Then he explained how he
heard teachers' secrets with his transistor. "See. I can sometimes find
out things people don't want me to.
So can Chip. He just goes invisible
by taking his clothes off. It makes us
special."

"What's so special about eaves-dropping and making up stupid jokes that make me feel bad?" said Charlene.

Chip scratched his shirt. "I didn't mean to make you feel bad."

"You guys should be using your powers for good, not evil."

"Charlene, we're not superheroes," said Chip. Justin nodded his head.

"I know," said Charlene. "But Justin can read lips and not everybody can do that. And Chip, well, *you're* certainly different."

"Right. We could call ourselves Two Weirdos for Peace and Justice," said Chip.

Justin laughed.

Charlene didn't.

"We could help kids who are in trouble," she said. "I got it! We could call ourselves Invisible Inc. The company that rights wrongs."

"What's this 'we'? What can *you* do?"

"I'm the one who thought of it," said Charlene. "Besides, you need a girl in your club. It's the law."

"She may be right," said Justin.

That afternoon, they went to Chip's house to get organized. "We need business cards," said Charlene, "to let people know that we're ready to help them."

Justin sat down at Chip's computer. Charlene dictated.

Justin tapped in her words. He printed them out on a business card.

INVISIBLE INC.

WE RIGHT WRONGS.

COME TO US WITH YOUR PROBLEMS.

WE CAN HELP.

It floated in the air. Chip was holding it without gloves on.

"I think we should write it in real invisible ink," said Charlene, peering at it over Chip's shoulder.

"Yeah? And where do we find invisible ink?" asked Justin.

"In the refrigerator," said Charlene. "Lemon juice looks invisible when you write with it. But if you hold it next to something warm, it shows up."

"Neat!" said Chip and Justin together.

Chip went to the refrigerator. He moved some hot dogs out of the way to get to the lemons. "You know, guys, this is the first time since the accident that I haven't felt like a weirdo."

Suddenly, Charlene screamed. "One of your hot dogs is running away."

A raw hot dog floated inches above the floor.

"That's just Max," said Chip. Max was Chip's dog. "He fell into the pool with me," said Chip. "But see? Part of his tail didn't get dipped."

Justin could see a little brown spot of a tail.

Chunks of hot dog mixed with
dog saliva in midair. "Hey, this is
neat," said Charlene. "It's kind of
like a science experiment."

"It's kind of disgusting," said
Justin. He took the lemons from
Chip and started to squeeze out invisible ink. It took a lot of lemons,
but Invisible Inc. was now official.

CHAPTER THREE
A Salamander Hostage

Chip, Justin, and Charlene handed out their business cards before school the next day.

Keith Broder took one. He laughed at it. "It's a blank card."

"Hold it up to something warm," said Chip.

Keith held it close to a light bulb. "What's this Invisible Inc.? Kids can't be incorporated."

"Yes, they can. Can't they Mr. Gonshak?" said Charlene.

"I think it's very nice that you children are helping Chip," said Mr. Gonshak.

"We're not doing it to help Chip," said Justin impatiently. "Chip and me and Charlene. *We* help people in trouble."

"Chip, Charlene, and *I*," corrected Mr. Gonshak. "Class, I am still very upset that the ball is missing from the playground. If anybody knows anything about this, please tell me. The principal, Ms. Maccarone, and I will not rest until we find out who took that ball. That ball is school property."

Chip passed a note to Charlene and Justin.

Maybe that's our first case. Invisible Inc. will find the ball and SAVE THE DAY!

Charlene and Justin nodded.

Mary raised her hand. Mary almost never raised her hand.

Mr. Gonshak called on her.

"I have a confession to make," whispered Mary. "I did it."

"Did what?" asked Mr. Gonshak.

Mary looked at the floor. "I took the ball," Mary stammered.

Mr. Gonshak stared at her. "Mary, *you*? Where is it?"

Mary's eyes were wide. "I . . . uh . . . I stuck it with my pen and made a hole in it, and then I buried it. I don't remember where."

"Mary!" Mr. Gonshak exclaimed. "That was a terrible thing to do. And so unlike you. Why did you do it?"

Mary wouldn't answer.

"I want to see you after school," said Mr. Gonshak.

Chip wrote a note and passed it to Charlene and Justin. *There goes our case.*

Charlene wrote back. *No! I'm sure Mary didn't do it. She needs our help.*

Justin nodded.

So did Chip. But nobody could see.

At lunchtime, Invisible Inc. asked
Mary if they could talk to her.

"I don't think so," said Mary.
Charlene held one of their cards up
to a warm dish of macaroni. Slowly,
INVISIBLE INC. WE RIGHT WRONGS.
became clear.

"You need us," said Charlene.

"No! Leave me alone," said Mary.
She ran away.

"That's great," said Justin. "Our first customer runs away. Invisible Inc. scores a big fat zero."

"Follow her, Chip," said Charlene. "Something is wrong."

Chip slipped off his clothes and went invisible. He followed Mary.

He was gone quite a while. When he came back, he put his clothes back on. "You won't believe what that stinker Keith Broder is doing to Mary."

"What?" Justin and Charlene asked.

"Remember that salamander that Mary brought for show-and-tell?"

"Dingbat," said Justin.

"Doormat," said Chip. "Well, Keith stuck the ball with his pen, and Mary saw him. But he's holding Doormat hostage and making Mary take the blame."

"Oh, poor Dingbat," said Justin.

"It's not Dingbat. It's Doormat," said Charlene and Chip together.

"We can't let him get away with this," said Charlene. She started to march across the lunchroom to make Keith confess.

Justin grabbed her. "Wait," he said. "He'll just deny it. We've got to trap him."

"How?" asked Chip.

Justin tapped his transistor. "I've got a plan," he whispered.

CHAPTER FOUR
High Fives

"I want to talk to you," Justin said to Keith during recess.

"Yeah, you and who else? Is that invisible kid with you?" Keith asked.

"No, I'm alone," said Justin. Justin backed against the wall.

"How do I know Chip's not invisible right behind you?" said Keith.

"You've got me backed in a corner," said Justin. "If Chip were behind me, I'd be squashing him."

"I like squished chips," said Keith. "What do you want? Or can't you hear me. Do you want me to talk louder?"

"No," said Justin, tapping the transistor around his neck. "I can

hear you. I know the wrong person is getting the blame for ruining our ball. You did it."

"Did Mary tell you?" asked Keith.

Justin nodded, but didn't say anything.

"There's nothing you can do about it," said Keith. "Mary is never in trouble. Mr. Gonshak won't do anything to her. That's why I picked on her. But she's in big trouble now for telling you. She'll never get her salamander back."

Keith shoved Justin. He glared back at him. "Don't try to follow me," he warned.

Justin stayed where he was.

Last year the PTO had paid to have a giant sandbox built for the kindergartners. Keith went to the sandbox. He shoved a little of the top of the sand to the side. There was Mary's pet salamander in its cage. A ripped giant ball was underneath the cage.

Chip grabbed the salamander and ran.

"Hey!" shouted Keith. All he could see was a cage floating across the playground. Chip handed the cage to Mary. Mary's mouth opened into a big O. Doormat had just flown across the playground into her hands.

Justin ran up to Keith. "You picked on the wrong person, dodo. Everything you said to me is on tape. This isn't my transistor. It's a tape recorder."

"Why, you little twerp!" said Keith. He tried to grab the transistor from around Justin's neck.

Suddenly, invisible hands grabbed Keith.

Keith tried to punch Chip, but only got air.

"What's going on?" demanded Mr. Gonshak.

"Keith has something to say to you," said Charlene.

Keith crossed his arms over his chest. He shook his head.

Justin tapped the tape recorder around his neck. "Would you like me to play my tape for Mr. Gonshak?" he asked.

Mr. Gonshak looked down and saw the deflated ball. "What's *this* doing here?" he asked.

Keith sighed. He knew he was caught. "I did it," he said. "I was just playing with my pen, and it slipped. Mary didn't do it. She just said that to be nice." Mary stroked her salamander's cage.

"You're going straight to the principal's office," said Mr. Gonshak. He looked at Justin and Charlene. "I'm glad to finally know the truth. Maybe the ball can be fixed. Did you kids have anything to do with finding it?"

"Invisible Inc. saved the day," said Charlene.

Mr. Gonshak smiled. He took Keith to the principal's office.

Chip came back with his baseball cap and his clothes on. He was breathing hard. His shirt went in and out.

"I don't know how to thank you," said Mary in a shy voice.

Justin grinned. "Just speak up," he said. "It's hard for me to hear you when you mumble."

"And always remember to call on Invisible Inc. when help is nowhere to be seen," said Charlene.

Justin and Chip tried to give each other a high five, but they missed each other's hands.

Finally their hands touched, and they gave each other a big hand-shake. "There's still work to be done," said Charlene, putting her hand on top of Justin's.

"Yeah," said Justin. "We've got to work on our high fives. It's hard to give a high five to an invisible hand."

"Nothing's too hard for Invisible Inc.," said Charlene.

Justin grinned. He couldn't see it, but he was sure that Chip was grinning, too.